G. F. Monkshood

Woman and Her Wits

Epigrams on Woman, Love, and Beauty

G. F. Monkshood

Woman and Her Wits
Epigrams on Woman, Love, and Beauty

ISBN/EAN: 9783337364588

Printed in Europe, USA, Canada, Australia, Japan

Cover: Foto ©Andreas Hilbeck / pixelio.de

More available books at **www.hansebooks.com**

Woman and the Wits

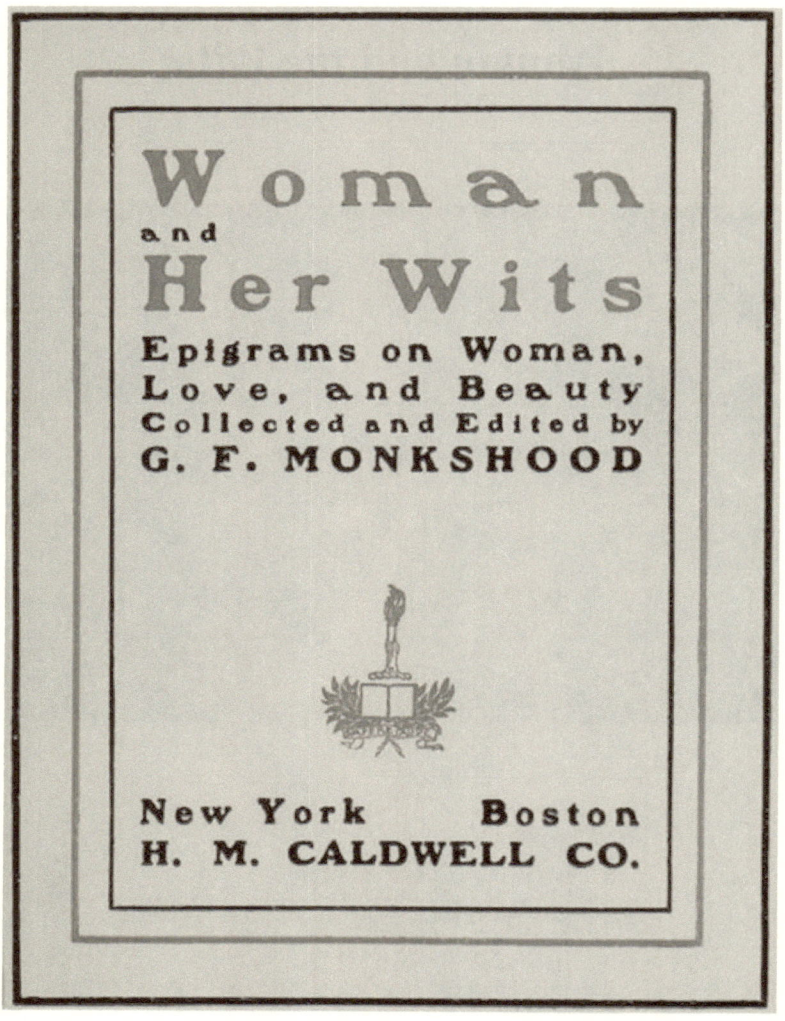

Woman
and
Her Wits

Epigrams on Woman,
Love, and Beauty
Collected and Edited by
G. F. MONKSHOOD

New York   Boston
H. M. CALDWELL CO.

———————————————

Dedicated
TO
R. R.
WITH HOMAGE.

G. F. M.

LONDON, 1899.

———————————————

PREFACE

Until some fortunate being — wit, student, and man of the world (he will have to be all three) — can, in a cunningly chosen library, write the history of the Epigram, and the birth and growth of epigrammatic thought, we shall always be in doubt as to what an epigram is, and most people will be in doubt as to where the best epigrams are. The word itself is as difficult to define as its own essences — wit, humour, style, etc. We recognise the epigram when uttered or printed just as swiftly as we recognise beauty in a woman, yet rarely can we describe either. The sheer study that awaits the historian of the Epigram has, doubtless, been a great deterrent; he would have to consider epigrams from the Bible and the apocryphal writings downwards! In "Woman and the Wits" I have brought together some of the wisest, wittiest, and tenderest epigrams, proverbs, axioms, adages or short, pithy sentences — call them what you will — relating to the woman and women, and also to the passions, affections, sentiments, and emotions generally.

My thanks are due principally to Mr. Morton and Mr. Du Bois for many excellent epigrams and for hints as to arrangement.

G. F. MONKSHOOD.

London, 1899.

Woman and the Wits

Second thoughts are best. God created man; woman was the after-thought.

Proverb.

I have been ready to believe that we have seen a new revelation, and the name of its Messiah is woman.

Holmes.

The whisper of a beautiful woman can be heard further than the loudest call of duty.

Anonymous.

The man who enters his wife's dressing-room is either a philosopher or a fool.

Balzac.

Be circumspect in your liaisons with women. It is better to be seen at the opera with this man than to be seen at mass with that woman.

Mme. de Maintenon.

Two women placed together make cold weather.

Shakespeare.

————————

I have seen many instances of women running to waste and self-neglect, and disappearing gradually from the earth, almost as if they had been exhaled to heaven.

Washington Irving.

————————

Physical love is an ephemeral spark designed to kindle in human hearts the flame of a more lasting love. It is the outer court of the temple.

Sabatier.

————————

Between the mouth and the kiss, there is always time for repentance.

Ricard.

————————

Love decreases when it ceases to increase.

Chateaubriand.

————————

Partake of love as a temperate man partakes of wine; do not become intoxicated.

De Musset.

A woman never commands a man, unless he be a fool, but by her obedience.

Turkish Spy.

Many benefit by the caresses they have not inspired; many a vulgar reality serves as a pedestal to an ideal idol.

Gautier.

In the highest society, as well as in the lowest, woman is merely an instrument of pleasure.

Tolstoi.

Women know at first sight the character of those with whom they converse. There is much to give them a religious height to which men do not attain.

Emerson.

Women see through and through each other; and often we most admire her whom they most scorn.

Buxton.

Woman is a miracle of divine contradictions.

Michelet.

Before going to war say a prayer; before going to sea say two prayers; before marrying say three prayers.

Proverb.

If marriages are made in Heaven you had but few friends there.

Scotch Proverb.

A man should choose for a wife only such a woman as he would choose for a friend, were she a man.

Joubert.

I think Nature and an angry God produced thee to the world, thou wicked sex, to be a plague to man.

Ariosto.

Women enjoy more the pleasure they give than the pleasure they feel.

Rochepedre.

Woman's tongue is her sword, which she never lets rust.

Mme. Necker.

Wife and children are a kind of discipline of humanity.

Bacon.

Feminine charity renews every day the miracle of Christ feeding a multitude with a few loaves and fishes.

Legouvé.

On seeing a lady sitting at the dinner-table between two Bishops, Sydney Smith inquired, "Her name is Susanna, I assume?"

With cleverness, thirty years, and a little beauty, a woman makes fewer conquests but more durable ones.

Dupuy.

Women who marry seldom act but once; their lot is, ere they wed, obedience unto a father, thenceforth to a husband.

Marston.

It is woman's way. They always love colour better than form, rhetoric better than logic, priestcraft better than philosophy, and flourishes better than figures.

Anonymous.

A prude exhibits her virtue in word and manner; a virtuous woman shows hers in her conduct.

La Bruyère.

Tears are the strength of women.

Saint-Evremond.

A woman's best qualities do not reside in her intellect, but in her affections. She gives refreshment by her sympathies rather than by her knowledge.

Smiles.

A woman's thoughts run before her actions.

Shakespeare.

It is valueless to a woman to be young unless pretty, or to be pretty unless young.

La Rochefoucauld.

Silence and modesty are the best ornaments of women.

Euripides.

The plainest man who pays attention to women will sometimes succeed as well as the handsomest who does not.

Colton.

A woman can be held by no stronger tie than the knowledge that she is loved.

Mme. de Motteville.

As vivacity is the gift of women, gravity is that of men.

Addison.

Women are passive agents, and when love prompts them they can outsuffer martyrs.

Massinger.

Between two beings susceptible to love, the duration of love depends upon the first resistance of the woman, or the obstacles that society puts in their way.

Balzac.

A woman (of the right kind) reading after a man, follows him as Ruth followed the reapers of Boaz, and her gleanings are often the finest of the wheat.

Holmes.

To a woman of spirit, the most intolerable of all grievances is a restraint on the liberty of the tongue.

Junius.

If women were humbler men would be honester.

Vanbrugh.

These women are shrewd tempters with their tongues.

Shakespeare.

———————————

Nature makes fools; women make coxcombs.

Anonymous.

———————————

No friendship is so cordial or so delicious as that of girl for girl; no hatred so intense or immovable as that of woman for woman.

Landor.

———————————

Women are priestesses of the unknown.

Anonymous.

———————————

To give you nothing and to make you expect everything, to dawdle on the threshold of love while the doors are closed, this is all the science of a coquette.

De Bernard.

———————————

Men always say more evil of a woman than there really is; and there is always more than is known.

Mezeray.

Neither walls, nor goods, nor anything is more difficult to be guarded than woman.

Alexis.

Would you hurt a woman most, aim at her affections.

Wallace.

A wise man ought often to admonish his wife, to reprove her seldom, but never to lay hands on her.

Marcus Aurelius.

A woman of honour should never suspect another of things she would not do herself.

Marguerite de Valois.

We only demand that a woman should be womanly; which is not being exclusive.

Leigh Hunt.

Man forsakes Christianity in his labours; woman

cherishes it in her solitudes and trials. Man lives by repelling, woman by enduring—and here Christianity meets her.

Channing.

It is not easy to be a widow; one must resume all the modesty of girlhood, without being allowed even to feign ignorance.

Mme. de Girardin.

A woman's hopes are woven as sunbeams; a shadow annihilates them.

George Eliot.

Women cannot see so far as men can, but what they do see they see quicker.

Buckle.

The more idle a woman's hand, the more occupied her heart.

Dubay.

Women speak easily of platonic love; but while they appear to esteem it highly, there is not a single ribbon of their toilet that does not drive platonism from our hearts.

Ricard.

If woman did turn man out of Paradise, she has done her best ever since to make it up to him.

Sheldon.

A man cannot possess anything that is better than a good woman, nor anything that is worse than a bad one.

Simonides.

A virtuous woman is a crown to her husband; but she that maketh ashamed is as rottenness in his bones.

Solomon.

How wisely it is constituted that tender and gentle women shall be our earliest guides—instilling their own spirits.

Channing.

Let woman stand upon her female character as upon a foundation.

Lamb.

The modest virgin, the prudent wife, and the careful matron are much more serviceable in life than petticoated philosophers, blustering characters, or virago queens.

Goldsmith.

A heart which has been domesticated by matrimony and maternity is as tranquil as a tame bullfinch.

Holmes.

If men knew all that women think, they would be twenty times more audacious.

Karr.

A beautiful woman pleases the eye, a good woman pleases the heart; one is a jewel, the other a treasure.

Napoleon I.

Women especially are to be talked to as below men and above children.

Chesterfield.

When joyous, a woman's licence is not to be endured; when in terror, she is a plague.

Æschylus.

Modesty in woman is a virtue most deserving, since we do all we can to cure her of it.

Lingrés.

When we speed to the devil's house, woman takes the lead by a thousand steps.

Goethe.

When a woman pronounces the name of a man but twice a day, there may be some doubt as to the nature of her sentiments; but three times!

Balzac.

Women know by nature how to disguise their emotions

far better than the most consummate male courtier can do.

Thackeray.

Beauty is worse than wine; it intoxicates both the holder and the beholder.

Zimmerman.

Woman alone knows true loyalty of affection.

Schiller.

Women are never stronger than when they arm themselves with their weakness.

Mme. du Deffand.

Women are apt to see chiefly the defects of a man of talent and the merits of a fool.

Anonymous.

Women have a perpetual envy of our vices; they are less vicious than we, not from choice, but because we restrict them; they are the slaves of order and fashion.

Johnson.

It is generally a feminine eye that first detects the moral deficiencies hidden under the "dear deceit" of beauty.

George Eliot.

I detest those women who mount the pulpit and lay their passions bare.

Eugenie de Guérin.

Of all men, Adam was the happiest; he had no mother-in-law.

Parfait.

Beloved darlings, who cover over and shadow many malicious purposes with a counterfeit passion of dissimulate sorrow and unquietness.

Sir Walter Raleigh.

A mother's tenderness and caresses are the milk of the heart.

Eugenie de Guérin.

Lovers have in their language an infinite number of words in which each syllable is a caress.

Rochepedre.

To love is the least of the faults of a loving woman.

La Rochefoucauld.

What is it that renders friendship between women so lukewarm and of so short a duration? It is the interests of love and the jealousy of conquest.

Rousseau.

There is nothing in love but what we imagine.

St Beuve.

I am a strenuous advocate for liberty and property, but when these rights are invaded by a pretty woman, I am neither able to defend my money nor my freedom.

Junius.

There are more people who wish to be loved than there are who are willing to love.

Chamfort.

––––––––––––––––––

To educate a man is to form an individual who leaves nothing behind him; to educate a woman is to form future generations.

Laboulaye.

––––––––––––––––––

There are no women to whom virtue comes easier than those who possess no attractions.

Anonymous.

––––––––––––––––––

In courting women, many dry wood for a fire that will not burn for them.

Balzac.

––––––––––––––––––

It is no more possible to do without a wife than it is to dispense with eating and drinking.

Luther.

––––––––––––––––––

God created the coquette as soon as he made the fool.

Victor Hugo.

The sweetest thing in life is the unclouded welcome of a wife.

Willis.

Trust not a woman, even when dead.

Latin Proverb.

I have seen more than one woman drown her honour in the clear water of diamonds.

Comtesse d'Houdetot.

Who trusts himself to woman or to waves should never hazard what he fears to lose.

Oldmixon.

It is vanity that renders the youth of women culpable and their old age ridiculous.

Mme. dé Sonza.

There are three things that women throw away—their time, their money, and their health.

Madame Geoffrin.

The pleasant man a woman will desire for her own sake, but the languishing lover has nothing to hope from but her pity.

Steele.

Woman is an overgrown child that one amuses with toys, intoxicates with flattery, and seduces with promises.

Sophie Arnould.

True modesty protects a woman better than her garments.

Anonymous.

Woman is the sweetest present that God has given to man.

Guyard.

Coquetry is the desire to please, without the want of love.

Rochepedre.

———————————

Before marriage, woman is a queen; after marriage, a subject.

De Maintenon.

———————————

Coquetry is a continual lie, which renders a woman more contemptible and more dangerous than a courtesan who never lies.

De Varennes.

———————————

The test of civilisation is the estimate of woman.

Curtis.

———————————

Provided a woman be well-principled she has dowry enough.

Plautus.

———————————

The more women have risked, the more they are willing to sacrifice.

Duclos.

A flattered woman is always indulgent.

Chenier.

Beauty is the eye's food and the soul's sorrow.

German Proverb.

Some cunning men choose fools for their wives, thinking to manage them, but they always fail.

Johnson.

A termagant wife may, therefore, in some respects be considered a tolerable blessing.

Washington Irving.

Divination seems heightened to its highest power in woman.

Bronson Alcott.

Silence has been given to woman to better express her thoughts.

Desnoyers.

———————————————————

The society of women endangers men's morals and refines their manners.

Montesquieu.

———————————————————

Women are supernumerary when present, and missed when absent.

Portuguese Proverb.

———————————————————

The virtuous woman who falls in love is much to be pitied.

La Rochefoucauld.

———————————————————

A coquette is more occupied with the homage we refuse her than with what we bestow upon her.

Dupuy.

———————————————————

Women are extremists; they are either better or worse than men.

La Bruyère.

Woman is the crime of man. She has been his victim since Eden. She wears on her flesh the trace of six thousand years of injustice.

Pelletan.

Socrates studied under Aspasia, and Aspasia governed the world under the name of Pericles.

Houssaye.

The one who has read the book that is called woman knows more than the one who has grown pale in libraries.

Houssaye.

Woman is the eighth capital sin, but she is perhaps the fourth theological virtue.

Houssaye.

All passions are good when one masters them.

Rousseau.

Consideration for woman is the measure of a nation's progress in social life.

Gregoire.

There is something of woman in everything that pleases.

Dupaty.

No man has yet discovered the means of giving successfully friendly advice to women—not even to his own.

Balzac.

The anger of a woman is the greatest evil with which one can threaten enemies.

Chillon.

I would have a woman as true as death. At the first real lie that works from the heart outward, she should be tenderly chloroformed into a better world.

Holmes.

There is no jewel in the world so valuable as a chaste and virtuous woman.

Cervantes.

───────────

Nature has given to women fortitude enough to resist a certain time, but not enough to resist completely the inclination which they cherish.

Dorat.

───────────

Without woman the two extremes of life would be without succour, and the middle without pleasure.

Anonymous.

───────────

In all eras and all climes a woman of great genius or beauty has done what she chose.

Ouida.

───────────

He that hath wife and children hath given hostages to fortune; for they are impediments to great enterprises, either of virtue or mischief.

Bacon.

───────────

A woman would be in despair if Nature had formed her as fashion makes her appear.

Mdlle. de Lespinasse.

The resistance of a woman is not always a proof of her virtue, but more frequently of her experience.

Ninon de l'Enclos.

What a wilful, wayward thing is woman! Even in their best pursuits so loose of soul that every breath of passion shakes their frame.

Francis.

The love of woman is universally for one man. Even though degraded, half-unsexed, outcast, abandoned to despair, she inflexibly seeks her individual own.

Browne.

Rascal! That word on the lips of a woman, addressed to a too daring man, often means angel!

Anonymous.

Why should man, who is strong, always get the best of it, and be forgiven so much; and woman who is weak, get the worst and be forgiven so little?

Mrs W. K. Clifford.

———————

WOMEN. Their love first inspires the poet, and their praise is his best reward.

Holmes.

———————

Women have no worse enemies than women.

Duclos.

———————

With what hope can we endeavour to persuade the ladies that the time spent at the toilet is lost in vanity.

Johnson.

———————

A mother's prayers, silent and gentle, can never miss the road to the throne of all bounty.

Beecher.

———————

Venus always saves the lover whom she leads.

Delatouche.

A good-tempered woman, of the order yclept buxom, not only warrants a pair of expansive shoulders, but bespeaks our approbation of them.

Leigh Hunt.

Men love at first and most warmly; women love last and longest. This is natural enough; for nature makes women to be won and men to win.

Curtis.

What we call in men *wisdom* is in women prudence. It is a partiality to call one greater than the other.

Steele.

An undoubted, uncontested, conscious beauty is, of all women, the least sensible of flattery.

Chesterfield.

Women who have not fine teeth laugh only with their eyes.

Mme. de Rieux.

Women generally consider consequences in love, seldom in resentment.

Colton.

Woo the widow whilst she is in weeds.

German Proverb.

Wounds of the heart! your traces are bitter, slow to heal, and always ready to re-open.

De Musset.

The head is always the dupe of the heart.

La Rochefoucauld.

O women! you are very extraordinary children.

Diderot.

There are different kinds of love, but they have all the same aim: possession.

Roqueplan.

A man who can love deeply is never utterly contemptible.

Balzac.

If love gives wit to fools, it undoubtedly takes it from wits.

A. Karr.

The great defect in men is that they never put themselves in the place of the woman they judge.

Mme. D'Epinay.

There is not a love, however violent it may be, to which ambition and interest do not add something.

La Bruyère.

A man philosophises better than a woman on the human heart, but she reads the hearts of men better than he.

Rousseau.

What a woman should demand of a man in courtship,

or after it, is, first, respect for her, as she is a woman; and next to that, to be respected by him above all other women.

Lamb.

———————

A beautiful and chaste woman is the perfect workmanship of God, the true glory of angels, the rare miracle of earth, and the sole wonder of the world.

Hermes.

———————

Just corporeal enough to attest humanity, yet sufficiently transparent to let the celestial origin shine through.

Ruffini.

———————

If we wish to know the political and moral condition of a State, we must ask what rank women hold in it. Their influence embraces the whole of life.

Aimi Martin.

———————

A woman,—where can she put her hope in storms, if not in Heaven?

Mitchell.

———————

Woman's heart is like a lithographer's stone, — what is once written upon it cannot be rubbed out.

Thackeray.

The lives of a multitude of women all around us contain a large element of unsuccessful outward or inward ambitions, — vain attempts and prayers.

Alger.

An ideal type, in which meekness, gentleness, patience, humility, faith and love are the most prominent features, is not naturally male, but female.

Lecky.

Even though the wife be little, bow down to her in speaking.

Talmud.

The vainest woman is never thoroughly conscious of her own beauty till she is loved by the man who sets her own passion vibrating in return.

George Eliot.

'Tis a terrible thing that we cannot wish young ladies well without wishing them to become old women.

Johnson.

We men have no right to say it, but the omnipotence of Eve is in humility.

Emerson.

Rejected lovers need never despair! There are four-and-twenty hours in a day, and not a moment in the twenty-four in which a woman may not change her mind.

De Finod.

There are few husbands whom the wife cannot win in the long run by patience and love, unless they are harder than the rocks which the soft water penetrates in time.

Marguerite de Valois.

The only true and firm friendship is that between man and woman, because it is the only affection exempt from actual or possible rivalry.

41

A. Comte.

The yoke of love is sometimes heavier than that of all the virtues.

Montaigne.

Love is the poetry of the senses.

Balzac.

Love is the beginning, the middle and the end of everything.

Lacordaire.

Women are constantly the dupes, or the victims of their extreme sensitiveness.

Balzac.

When a man says he has a wife, it means that a wife has him.

Gavarni.

Woman is more constant in hatred than in love.

Anonymous.

A woman dies twice; the day that she quits life and the day that she ceases to please.

Weiss.

Love is the association of two beings for the benefit of one.

Countess Nathalie.

What a woman wills, God wills.

Proverb.

Some women kindle emotion so rapidly in a man's heart, that the judgment cannot keep pace with it.

Hardy.

The Bible says that woman is the last thing which God made. He must have made it on Saturday night. It shows fatigue.

Dumas.

Woman's power is for rule, not for battle; and her intellect is not for invention or creation, but for sweet ordering, arrangement and decision.

Ruskin.

Woman is a delightful musical instrument, of which love is the bow and man the artist.

Bayle.

Fit the same intellect to a man, and it is a bowstring; to a woman, and it is a harpstring.

Holmes.

A clip of a wife roasts her husband, stouthearted though he may be, without a fire, and hands him over to premature old age.

Hesiod.

There are three things I have always loved and have never understood—painting, music, and woman.

Fontenelle.

Learned women have lost all credit by their impertinent talkativeness and conceit.

Swift.

―――――――

The coquette compromises her reputation, and sometimes even her virtue; the prude, on the contrary, often sacrifices her honour in private, and preserves it in public.

Mme. du Boccage.

―――――――

When a woman has explicitly condemned a given action, she apparently gathers courage for its commission under a little different conditions.

Howells.

―――――――

The homage of a man may be delightful until he asks straight for love, by which woman renders homage.

George Eliot.

―――――――

The Divine Right of Beauty is the only one an Englishman ought to acknowledge, and a pretty woman is the only tyrant he is not authorised to resist.

Junius.

―――――――

The beauty of a lovely woman is like music.

George Eliot.

If there be any one whose power is in beauty, in purity, in goodness, it is woman.

Ward Beecher.

God created woman only to tame man.

Voltaire.

O woman! it is thou that causeth the tempests that agitate mankind.

Rousseau.

The laughter, the tears, and the song of a woman are equally deceptive.

Latin Proverb.

A woman's lot is made for her by the love she accepts.

George Eliot.

Woman is an idol that man worships until he throws it down.

Anonymous.

She who dresses for others besides her husband, marks herself a wanton.

Euripides.

With soft persuasive prayers woman wields the sceptre of the life which she charmeth.

Schiller.

Men are the cause of women's dislike for one another.

La Bruyère.

The beautiful woman always gives me joy, and a high mind, too, if I think what she does for me.

Reinmar.

Women have the genius of charity. A man gives but his

gold; a woman adds to it her sympathy.

Legouvé.

―――――――――

A woman's preaching is like a dog's walking on his hind legs. It is not done well, but you are surprised to find it done at all.

Johnson.

―――――――――

The only way to get the upper hand of a woman, is to be more woman than she is herself.

Anonymous.

―――――――――

The devastating egotism of man is properly foreign to woman; though there are many women as haughty, hard and imperious as any man.

Alger.

―――――――――

There are some women who think virtue was given them as claws were given to cats—to do nothing but scratch with.

Jerrold.

―――――――――

An immodest woman is food without salt.

Arabian Proverb.

———————————

The evil in women is usually communicated by men. Much of the deceit of which they are accused is the effect of masculine inoculation.

Browne.

———————————

The lover never sees personal resemblances in his mistress to her kindred or to others.

Emerson.

———————————

The friendship of a man is often a support; that of a woman is always a consolation.

Rochepedre.

———————————

Woman is the blood royal of life; let there be slight degrees of precedence among them, but let them all be sacred.

Burns.

———————————

The woman who is resolved to be respected can make

herself to be so, even amidst an army of soldiers.

Cervantes.

To form devices quick is woman's wit.

Euripides.

Woman's power is over the affections. A beautiful dominion is hers, but she risks its forfeiture when she seeks to extend it.

Bovée.

To remain virtuous, a man has only to combat his own desires; a woman must resist her own inclinations and the continual attack of man.

De Latena.

A cunning woman is a knavish fool.

Lyttleton.

A woman often thinks she regrets the lover, when she only regrets the love.

La Rochefoucauld.

Even the satyrs, like men, in one way or another, could win the love of a woman.

Malcolm Johnson.

You wish to create Eve over again, or rather to call forth a female Adam. I object.

Sheldon.

Let a man pray that none of his woman-kind should form a just estimation of him.

Thackeray.

In love, she who gives her portrait promises the original.

Dupuy.

The man who seems to care little whether he charms or attracts women is he who offends and seduces.

Goethe.

To correct the faults of man, we address the head; to correct those of woman, we address the heart.

De Beauchêne.

―――――――――――

The man flaps about with a bunch of feathers: the woman goes to work softly with a cloth.

Holmes.

―――――――――――

Glory can be for a woman but the brilliant mourning of happiness.

Mme. de Stael.

―――――――――――

Women have more of what is termed good sense than men. They cannot reason wrong, for they do not reason at all.

Hazlitt.

―――――――――――

In anger against a rival, all women, even duchesses, employ invective. Then they make use of everything as a weapon.

Anonymous.

―――――――――――

What is civilisation? I answer, the power of good women.

Emerson.

———————

Science seldom renders men amiable; women, never.

Beauchêne.

———————

The egotism of woman is always for two.

Mme. de Stael.

———————

The wisest woman you talk with is ignorant of something that you know, but an elegant woman never forgets her elegance.

Holmes.

———————

A widow is like a frigate of which the first captain has been shipwrecked.

Karr.

———————

Where women are, are all kinds of mischief.

Menander.

Woman is the symbol of moral and physical beauty.

Gautier.

No man knows what the wife of his bosom is—no man knows what a ministering angel she is—until he has gone with her through the fiery trials of this world.

Washington Irving.

Women have, in general, but one object, which is their beauty; upon which scarce any flattery is too gross for them.

Chesterfield.

If Cleopatra's nose had been shorter, the face of the whole world would have been changed.

Pascal.

A worthless girl has enslaved me,—me, whom no enemy ever did.

Epictetus.

An indigent female, the object probably of love and tenderness in her youth, at a more advanced age a withered flower, has nothing to do but retire and die.

Hall.

In love affairs, from innocence to the fault, there is but a kiss.

Alberic Second.

The destiny of women is to please, to be amiable, and to be loved.

Rochebrune.

A beautiful woman is the paradise of the eyes, the hell of the soul, and the purgatory of the purse.

Anonymous.

If you would make a pair of good shoes, take for the sole the tongue of a woman; it never wears out.

Alsatian Proverb.

One is always a woman's first lover.

————————————

A man must be a fool who does not succeed in making a woman believe that which flatters her.

Balzac.

————————————

I have seen faces of women that were fair to look upon, yet one could see that the icicles were forming round these women's hearts.

Holmes.

————————————

The highest mark of esteem a woman can give a man is to ask his friendship, and the most signal proof of her indifference is to offer him hers.

Anonymous.

————————————

The fire of woman's passion, consuming the wilderness of her limitation, rises to the pure flame that has blazed on every altar of Eros between the Nile and the Columbia.

Browne.

————————————

Frailty! thy name is woman.

Shakespeare.

The tears of a young widow lose their bitterness when wiped by the hands of love.

Anonymous.

She could not reconcile the anxieties of spiritual life, involving eternal consequences, with a keen interest in gimp and artificial protrusions of drapery.

George Eliot.

Venus herself, if she were bald, would not be Venus.

Apuleius.

Women often deceive to conceal what they feel; men to simulate what they do not feel—love.

Legouvé.

Women are the happiest beings of the creation; in compensation for our services, they reward us with a happiness of which they retain more than half.

De Varennes.

━━━━━━━━━━━━━━━━

No woman is too silly not to have a genius for spite.

Anonymous.

━━━━━━━━━━━━━━━━

There is no compensation for the woman who feels that the chief relation of her life has been a mistake. She has lost her crown.

George Eliot.

━━━━━━━━━━━━━━━━

There are plenty of women who believe women to be incapable of anything but to cook, incapable of interest in affairs.

Emerson.

━━━━━━━━━━━━━━━━

A woman is happy and attains all that she desires when she captivates a man; hence the great object of her life is to master the art of captivating men.

Tolstoi.

━━━━━━━━━━━━━━━━

The secret of youthful looks in an aged face is easy shoes, easy corsets and an easy conscience.

Anonymous.

━━━━━━━━━━━━━━━━

Who does not know the bent of woman's fancy?

Spenser.

━━━━━━━━━━━━━━━━

Love makes mutes of those who habitually speak most fluently.

De Souderi.

━━━━━━━━━━━━━━━━

Every great passion is but a prolonged hope.

Feuchères.

━━━━━━━━━━━━━━━━

Beauty in woman is power.

De Rotrou.

━━━━━━━━━━━━━━━━

We are by no means aware how much we are influenced by our passions.

La Rochefoucauld.

━━━━━━━━━━━━━━━━

To love is to admire with the heart; to admire is to love

with the mind.

Gautier.

Glances are the first *billets-doux* of love.

De L'Enclos.

Beauty and ugliness disappear equally under the wrinkles of age; one is lost in them, the other hidden.

Petit-Senn.

Where pride begins, love ends.

Lavater.

The girl who wakes the poet's sigh is a very different creature from the girl who makes his soup.

Sheldon.

Women know a point more than the devil.

Italian Proverb.

To a gentleman every woman is a lady in right of her sex.

Lytton.

Did you ever hear of a man's growing lean by the reading of "Romeo and Juliet," or blowing his brains out because Desdemona was maligned?

Holmes.

Great women belong to history and to self-sacrifice.

Leigh Hunt.

The heart of a coquette is like a rose, of which the lovers pluck the leaves, leaving only the thorns for the husband.

Anonymous.

In our age women commonly preserve the publication of their good offices and their vehement affection toward their husbands until they have lost them.

Montaigne.

61

When women cannot be revenged, they do as children do—they then cry.

Cardan.

————

At twenty, man is less a lover of woman than of women; he is more in love with the sex than with the individual, however charming she may be.

La Bretonne.

————

The man who has taken one wife deserves a crown of patience; the man who has taken two deserves two crowns of pity.

Proverb.

————

The knowledge of the charms one possesses prompts one to utilise them.

Sénancourt.

————

There is no more agreeable companion than the one woman who loves us.

St Pierre.

————

Jealousy is the sister of love, as the devil is the brother of the angels.

Boufflers.

Men bestow compliments only on women who deserve none.

Bachi.

Two smiles that approach each other end in a kiss.

Hugo.

There is in every true woman's heart a spark of heavenly fire, which beams and blazes in the dark hours of adversity.

Washington Irving.

A woman is never displeased if we please several other women, provided she is preferred. It is so many more triumphs for her.

Ninon de L'Enclos.

There is a woman at the beginning of all great things.

Lamartine.

Women prefer us to say a little evil of them, rather than to say nothing of them at all.

Ricard.

One syllable of woman's speech can dissolve more of love than a man's heart can hold.

Holmes.

———————————

Women, deceived by men, want to marry them; it is a kind of revenge, as good as any other.

Beaumanoir.

———————————

A woman is seldom tenderer to a man than immediately after she has deceived him.

Anonymous.

———————————

Women like balls and assemblies, as a hunter likes a place where game abounds.

De Latena.

———————————

Fortune rules in nuptials; women are as like to turn out badly as to prove a source of joy.

Euripides.

———————————

One of the sweetest pleasures of a woman is to cause

regret.

Chevalier.

―――――――――――――

Man without woman is head without body; woman without man is body without head.

German Proverb.

―――――――――――――

Wrinkles disfigure a woman less than ill-nature.

Dupuy.

―――――――――――――

I am sure I do not mean it an injury to women when I say there is a sort of sex in souls.

Steele.

―――――――――――――

A woman, when she has passed forty becomes an illegible scrawl; only an old woman is capable of divining old women.

Balzac.

―――――――――――――

A beautiful woman is never silly; she has the best wit that a man may ask of a woman, she is pretty.

Stahl.

All the reasons of men are not worth one sentiment of woman.

Voltaire.

A man never knows how to live until a woman has lived with him.

Mere.

It may not be impossible to find a constant heart in an unfaithful body.

Stahl.

Women may be pardoned for lack of common sense. The culprit in them is the heart.

Stahl.

The history of love would be the history of humanity; it would be a beautiful book to write.

Nodier.

Love is composed of so many sensations, that something new of it can always be said.

Saint Prosper.

A woman is frank when she is not uselessly untruthful.

France.

Jealousy for a woman is only a wound to self-respect. In man it is a torture profound as moral suffering, continuous as physical suffering.

France.

Love preserves beauty, and the flesh of woman is fed with caresses as are bees with flowers.

France.

Every lover who tries to find in love anything else than love is not a lover.

Bourget.

One must be sensual to be human.

France.

When a lover gives, he demands—and much more than he has given.

Parry.

In most men there is a dead poet whom the man survives.

St Beuve.

The Egyptian people, wisest then of nations, gave to their Spirit of Wisdom the form of a woman; and into her hand, for a symbol, the weaver's shuttle.

Ruskin.

The life of a woman can be divided into three epochs; in the first she dreams of love, in the second she experiences it, in the third she regrets it.

Saint Prosper.

The ruses of women multiply with their years.

Proverb.

Women wish to be loved, not because they are pretty or good or well-bred or graceful or intelligent, but because they are themselves.

Amiel.

———————————

Society depends upon women. The nations who confine them are unsociable.

Voltaire.

———————————

A beautiful woman with the qualities of a noble man is the most perfect thing in nature.

La Bruyère.

———————————

Woman, in accordance with her unbroken, clear-seeing nature, loses herself and what she has of heart and happiness in the object she loves.

Richter.

———————————

Society is the book of women.

Rousseau.

———————————

Women, like princes, find few real friends.

Lyttleton.

In love affairs, a young shepherdess is a better partner than an old queen.

De Finod.

To "Get out of my house," and "What do you want with my wife?" there is no answer.

Don Quixote.

Our ice-eyed brain women are really admirable if we only ask of them just what they can give, and no more.

Holmes.

A marriageable girl is a kind of merchandise that can be negotiated at wholesale only on condition that no one takes a part at retail.

Karr.

Woman is a flower that exhales her perfume only in the shade.

De Lamennais.

An honest woman is the one we fear to compromise.

Balzac.

A woman, the more curious she is about her face, is commonly the more careless about her home.

Ben Jonson.

Heaven has refused genius to woman, in order to concentrate all the fire in her heart.

Rivarol.

The two pleasantest days of a woman are her marriage day and the day of her funeral.

Hipponax.

A woman who writes commits two sins; she increases the number of books, and decreases the number of women.

Karr.

A lady's wish—he said, with a certain gallantry of manner—makes slaves of us all.

Holmes.

In nineteen cases out of twenty, for a woman to play her heart in the game of love is to play at cards with a sharper, and gold coin against counterfeit pieces.

Bourget.

Women are at ease in perfidy, as are serpents in bushes.

Feuillet.

Women see without looking; their husbands often look without seeing.

Desnoyers.

Most women who ride well on horseback have little tenderness. Like the Amazons, they lack a breast.

Anonymous.

Earth has nothing more tender than a woman's heart when it is the abode of pity.

Luther.

In wishing to control her empire, woman destroys it.

Canabis.

Wherever women are honoured, the gods are satisfied.

Laws of Manu.

To a woman, the romances she makes are more amusing than those she reads.

Gautier.

Women give themselves to God when the devil wants nothing more with them.

Sophie Arnould.

Sensualism intrudes into the education of young women, and withers the hope and affection of human nature.

Emerson.

All the reasoning of man is not worth one sentiment of woman.

Voltaire.

When an old crone frolics, she flirts with death.

Syrus.

There never was in any age such a wonder to be found as a dumb woman.

Plautus.

Wives are young men's mistresses, companions for middle age, and old men's nurses.

Bacon.

Tenderness has no deeper source than the heart of a woman, devotion no purer shrine, sacrifice no more saint-like abnegation.

Saint-Foix.

It is difficult for a woman to keep a secret; and I know more than one man who is a woman.

———————————

All the evil that women have done to us comes from us, and all the good they have done to us comes from them.

Aimi Martin.

———————————

Have a useful and good wife in the house, or don't marry at all.

Euripides.

———————————

There are beautiful flowers that are scentless, and beautiful women that are unlovable.

Houelle.

———————————

None can do a woman worse despite than to call her old.

Ariosto.

———————————

He who flatters women most pleases them best, and they are most in love with him whom they think is most in love with them.

Chesterfield.

Suitors of a wealthy girl seldom seek for proof of her past virtue.

Anonymous.

Imperious Venus is less potent than caressing Venus.

Anonymous.

The clown knows very well that the women are not in love with him, but with Hamlet, the fellow in the black cloak and plumed hat.

Holmes.

Do you not know I am a woman? When I think, I must speak.

Shakespeare.

Women, asses, and nuts require strong hands.

Italian Proverb.

Woman sends forth her sympathies on adventure. She

embarks her whole soul in the traffic of affection; and if shipwrecked, her case is hopeless.

Washington Irving.

A woman is sometimes fugitive, irrational, indeterminable, illogical and contradictory. A great deal of forbearance ought to be shown her.

Amiel.

What a strange illusion it is to suppose that beauty is goodness! A beautiful woman utters absurdities: we listen, and we hear not the absurdities but wise thoughts.

Tolstoi.

A woman cannot guarantee her heart, even though her husband be the greatest and most perfect of men.

George Sand.

It is born in maidens that they should wish to please everything that has eyes.

Gleim.

The woman who throws herself at a man's head will soon find her place at his feet.

Desnoyers.

Women and wine, game and deceit, make the wealth small and the wants great.

Proverb.

I confess I like the quality ladies better than the common kind even of literary ones.

Holmes.

Women sometimes deceive the lover—never the friend.

Mercier.

You see in no place of conversation the perfection of speech so much as in accomplished women.

Steele.

A fan is indispensable to a woman who can no longer blush.

Anonymous.

79

When a wrong idea possesses a woman, much bitterness flows from her tongue.

Euripides.

Marriage communicates to women the vices of men, but never their virtues.

Fourier.

In love, the confidant of a woman's sorrow often becomes the consoler of it.

Anonymous.

A royal court without women is like a year without spring, a spring without flowers.

Francis I. of France.

A woman full of faith in the one she loves is but a novelist's fancy.

Balzac.

O Pygmalion, who can wonder (no artist surely) that thou didst fall in love with the work of thine own hands.

Leigh Hunt.

The mistakes of a woman result almost always from her faith in the good and her confidence in the truth.

Balzac.

Let an action be never so trivial in itself, women always make it appear of the most importance.

Pope.

There are only two beautiful things in the world— women and roses; and only two sweet things—women and melons.

Malherbe.

Before promising a woman to love only her, one should have seen them all, or should see only her.

Dupuy.

Many young girls have a strange audacity blended with their instinctive delicacy.

Holmes.

———————————————

Friendship that begins between a man and a woman will soon change its name.

Anonymous.

———————————————

The happiest women, like the happiest nations, have no history.

George Eliot.

———————————————

Women are formed by nature to feel some consolation in present troubles, by having them always in their mouth and on their tongue.

Euripides.

———————————————

Women give entirely to their affections, set their whole fortunes on the die, lose themselves eagerly in the glory of their husbands and children.

Emerson.

———————————————

We ask four things for a woman—that virtue dwell in her heart, modesty in her forehead, sweetness in her mouth, and labour in her hands.

Chinese Proverb.

In all ill-matched marriages, the fault is less the woman's than the man's, as the choice depended on her the least.

Mme. de Rieux.

Love lessens the woman's refinement and strengthens the man's.

Richter.

Who takes an eel by the tail, or a woman at her word, soon finds he holds nothing.

Proverb.

Homeliness is the best guardian of a young girl's virtue.

Mme. de Genlis.

In condemning the vanity of women, men complain of

the fire they themselves have kindled.

Lingrée.

———————————

A prude ought to be condemned to meet only indiscreet lovers.

Raisson.

———————————

Women always speak the truth, but not the whole truth.

Italian Proverb.

———————————

If all women's faces were cast in the same mould, that mould would be the grave of love.

Bichat.

———————————

What colour would it not have given to my thoughts, and what thrice-washed whiteness to my words, had I been fed on woman's praises.

Holmes.

———————————

One may see the heart of women through the rents which one may make in their self-love.

———————————

Women and music should never be dated.

Goldsmith.

———————————

Men never are consoled for their first love, nor women for their last.

Weiss.

———————————

A timorous woman often drops into her grave before she is done deliberating.

Addison.

———————————

It is much worse to irritate an old woman than a dog.

Menander.

———————————

There are women so hard to please that it seems as if nothing less than an angel will suit them; hence it comes that they often meet with devils.

Marguerite de Valois.

———————————

Woman is a charming creature, who changes her heart as easily as her gloves.

Balzac.

———————————

Women go further in love than most men, but men go further in friendship than women.

La Bruyère.

———————————

Woman's function is a guiding, not a determining one.

Ruskin.

———————————

At first woman fosters our dearest hopes with the affection of a mother; then, like a giddy hen she forsakes the nest.

Goethe.

———————————

A girl of sixteen accepts love; a woman of thirty incites it.

Ricard.

———————————

A woman who loves, however erring, can never be entirely selfish, for love has a humanising influence, and a true passion renders any self-sacrifice easy.

Peabody.

A secret passion defends the heart of a woman better than her moral sense.

De La Bretonne.

Women's hearts are made of stout leather; there's a plaguey sight of wear in them.

Haliburton.

A woman who pretends to laugh at love is like the child who sings at night when he is afraid.

Rousseau.

Woman among savages is a beast of burden; in Asia she is a piece of furniture; in Europe she is a spoiled child.

De Meilhan.

Women that are least bashful are not infrequently the most modest.

Colton.

True feeling is a rustic vulgarity the flirt does not tolerate; she counts its healthiest and most honest manifestation all sentiment.

Mitchell.

Shakespeare has no heroes, he has only heroines.

Ruskin.

Some men are different; all women are alike.

Delvau.

The empire of woman is an empire of sweetness, skilfulness and attractiveness; her orders are caresses, her evils are tears.

Rousseau.

Women need not be beautiful every day of their lives; it is sufficient that they have moments which one does not forget, and the return of which one expects.

Cherbuliez.

There are some lips from which even the proudest women love to hear the censure which appears to disprove indifference.

Lytton.

It is in the nature of the feminine sex to seek here below to corrupt men, and therefore wise men never abandon themselves to the seductions of women.

Laws of Manu.

Would that the race of women had never existed— except for me alone!

Euripides.

Fools that on women trust; for in their speech is death, hell in their smile.

Tasso.

At the age of sixty, to marry a beautiful girl of sixteen is to imitate those ignorant people who buy books to be read by their friends.

Ricard.

Women forgive injuries, but never forget slights.

Haliburton.

The virtue of women is often the love of reputation and quiet.

Rochefoucauld.

Woman is the most precious jewel taken from Nature's casket for the ornamentation and happiness of man.

Guyard.

Women have such a wonderful power of secreting adjectives that they cannot speak the truth when they try.

Sheldon.

Women divine that they are loved long before it is told them.

Marivaux.

The nervous fluid in man is consumed by the brain, in woman by the heart; it is there that they are most sensitive.

Bayle.

There will always remain something to be said of woman, as long as there is one on the earth.

De Boufflers.

The virtue of widows is a laborious virtue; they have to combat constantly with the remembrance of past bliss.

Jerome.

A woman whose ruling passion is not vanity is superior to any man of equal capacity.

Lavater.

Woman's natural mission is to love, to love but one, to love always.

Michelet.

One reason why women are forbidden to preach the gospel is that they would persuade without argument and reprove without giving offence.

John Newton.

How little do lovely women know what awful beings they are in the eyes of inexperienced youth.

Washington Irving.

During their youth women wish to be treated as divinities; they adore the ideal; they cannot bear the idea of being what Nature wishes them to be.

Anonymous.

Love is a bird that sings in the heart of a woman.

Karr.

Woman's happiness is in obeying. She objects to men who abdicate too much.

Michelet.

Nature sent woman into the world with the bridal dower of love.

Richter.

The moral amelioration of man constitutes the chief mission of women.

Comte.

Most ladies who have had what is considered as an education, have no idea of an education progressive through life.

Foster.

One of the principal occupations of men is to divine women.

Lacretelle.

Men do not always love those they esteem; women, on the contrary, esteem only those they love.

Dubay.

I will not affirm that women have no character; rather, they have a new one every day.

Heine.

The only person who can cure one of a woman is that woman herself.

Anonymous.

Virtue is a beautiful thing in women when they don't go about with it like a child with a drum, making all sorts of noise with it.

Jerrold.

Wiles and deceits are woman's specialities.

Æschylus.

What man seeks in love is woman; what woman seeks in love is man.

Houssaye.

There is no grace that is taught by the dancing-master, no style adopted into the etiquette of courts, but was first the whim and mere action of some brilliant woman.

Emerson.

The conversation of women in society resembles the straw used in packing china; it is nothing, yet without it, everything would be broken.

Mme. de Salm.

The woman who does not choose to love should cut the matter short at once by holding out no hope to her suitor.

Marguerite de Valois.

One single honest man may yet be seen; but wander all the world round to find one honest woman, he will search in vain.

Wieland.

A woman forgives the audacity which her beauty has prompted us to be guilty of.

Lesage.

To marry a wife, if we regard the truth, is an evil, but it is a necessary evil.

Menander.

Nothing is more difficult to choose than a good husband—unless it be to choose a good wife.

Rousseau.

The rudest man, inspired by love, is more persuasive than the most eloquent man, if uninspired.

La Rochefoucauld.

One of the sweetest pleasures of a woman is to cause regret.

Gavarni.

Constancy is the chimera of love.

Vauvenargues.

The pretension of youth always gives to a woman a few more years than she really has.

Jouy.

I have only one advice to give you—fall in love with all women.

Montmarin.

A beautiful face is the most beautiful of all spectacles.

La Bruyère.

The sweetest harmony is the sound of the voice of the woman one loves.

La Bruyère.

To marry is to domesticate the Recording Angel!

R. L. Stevenson.

When one writes of woman he must reserve the right to laugh at his ideas of the day before.

Ricard.

Who hath a fair wife hath need of more than two eyes.

Proverb.

Men bestow compliments only on women who deserve none.

Mme. Bachi.

Woman is more the companion of her own thoughts and feelings, and if they are turned to ministers of sorrow, where shall she look for consolation?

Washington Irving.

Vanity, shame and, above all, temperament often makes the valour of men and the virtue of women.

La Rochefoucauld.

Bachelors are providential beings; God created them for the consolation of widows and the hope of maids.

De Finod.

As the faculty of writing is chiefly a masculine endowment, the reproach of making the world miserable has been always thrown upon the women.

Johnson.

We look at one little woman's face we love, as we look at the face of our mother earth, and see all sorts of answers to our yearnings.

George Eliot.

There are some women who seem cold and beautiful stones, their hearts icicles, their tears frozen gems pressed out by injured pride.

Alger.

Position, Wren said, is essential to the perfecting of beauty—a fine building is lost in a dark lane; a statue should be in the air; much more true is it of woman.

Emerson.

A woman should never accept a lover without the consent of her heart, nor a husband without the consent of her judgment.

De Lenclos.

Most women spend their lives in robbing the old tree from which Eve plucked the first fruit.

Feuillet.

What is it that love does to women? Without it, she only sleeps; with it alone, she lives.

Ouida.

Female levity is no less fatal to them after marriage than before.

Addison.

The highest dressers, the highest face-painters, are not the loveliest women, but such as have lost their loveliness, or never had any.

Leigh Hunt.

The heart of a woman never grows old; when it has ceased to love it has ceased to live.

Rochepedre.

Neither in adversity nor in the joys of prosperity let me be associated with woman-kind.

Æschylus.

Women ask if a man is discreet, as men ask if a woman is pretty.

Anonymous.

It is only the coward who reproaches as a dishonour the love a woman has cherished for him.

Mme. de Lambert.

There is scarcely a single cause in which a woman is not engaged in some way fomenting the suit.

Juvenal.

Do not take women from the bedside of those who suffer; it is their post of honour.

Mme. Fée.

It is lucky for the poets that their mistresses are not obliged to sit to them. They would never write a line.

Leigh Hunt.

It is easier for a woman to defend her virtue against men than her reputation against women.

Rochebrune.

Twice is a woman dear—when she comes to the house and when she leaves it.

Anonymous.

———————————————

A woman is like your shadow; follow her, she flies; fly from her, she follows.

Proverb.

———————————————

Woman is a changeable thing, as our Virgil informed us at school; but her change *par excellence* is from the fairy you woo to the brownie you wed.

Lytton.

———————————————

How many ways to the heart has a woman?

Channing.

———————————————

What manly eloquence could produce such an effect as woman's silence.

Michelet.

———————————————

When maidens sue, men live like gods.

Proverb.

———————————————

I think it takes a great deal from a woman's modesty, going into public life; and modesty is her greatest charm.

Mrs Ward Beecher.

━━━━━━━━━━━━━━━

The passion for praise, which is so very vehement in the fair sex, produces excellent effects in women of sense.

Addison.

━━━━━━━━━━━━━━━

With women, friendship ends when rivalry begins.

Anonymous.

━━━━━━━━━━━━━━━

A woman is easily governed if a man takes her hand.

La Bruyère.

━━━━━━━━━━━━━━━

The lover cannot paint his maiden to his fancy poor and solitary.

Emerson.

━━━━━━━━━━━━━━━

The man who can govern a woman can govern a nation.

Balzac.

An old woman is a very bad bride, but a very good wife.

Fielding.

Apelles used to paint a good housewife on a snail, to import that she was a home-keeper.

Howell.

Man argues woman may not be trusted too far; woman feels man cannot be trusted too near.

Browne.

Nature has hardly formed a woman ugly enough to be insensible to flattery upon her person.

Chesterfield.

God has placed the genius of women in their hearts, because the works of this genius are always works of love.

Lamartine.

To think of the part one little woman can play in the life of a man, so that to renounce her may be a very good imitation of heroism, and to win her may be a discipline!

George Eliot.

The truth is, women are lost because they do not deliberate.

Amelia E. Barr.

When God thought of *Mother*, he must have laughed with satisfaction, and framed it quickly, so rich, so deep, so divine, so full of soul, power and beauty was the conception.

Ward Beecher.

A woman may always help her husband by what she knows, however little; by what she half knows, or mis-knows, she will only tease him.

Ruskin.

Diffuse knowledge generally among women, and you will at once cure the conceit which knowledge occasions while it is rare.

Sydney Smith.

―――――――――

The love of woman has in all ages given birth in man to passionate desires, poetic dreams, deferential attentions, persuasive forms of politeness.

Alger.

―――――――――

A lady who had not learned discretion by experience and came to an evil end.

Holmes.

―――――――――

In the elevated order of ideas, the life of man is glory; the life of woman is love.

Balzac.

―――――――――

Women have more strength in their looks than we have in our laws, and more power by their tears than we have by our arguments.

Saville.

―――――――――

The path of a good woman is indeed strewn with

flowers; but they rise behind her steps, not before them. "Her feet have touched the meadows and left the daisies rosy."

Ruskin.

The masculine personal pronoun is singularly restricted in woman's judgment. Passion has curtailed her grammar amazingly. She can remember only one number (that is Greek).

Browne.

There is nothing sadder than to look at dressy old things, who have reached the frozen latitudes beyond fifty, and who persist in appearing in the airy costume of the tropics.

Sheldon.

A woman finds it a much easier task to do an evil than a virtuous deed.

Plautus.

I have always said it: Nature meant to make woman its masterpiece.

Lessing.

Woman is the organ of the devil.

De Varennes.

Women are a breed the like of which neither sea nor earth produces anything; he who is always with them knows them best.

Euripides.

Women make us lose paradise, but how frequently we find it again in their arms.

De Finod.

Marriage has its unknown great men as war has its Napoleons, poetry its Cheniers, and philosophy its Descartes.

Balzac.

Vanity ruins more women than love.

Du Deffand.

Extremes in everything is a characteristic of woman.

De Goncourt.

One loves more the first time, better the second.

Rochepedre.

Of all religions love is the most deceptive.

Paleologue.

The Indian axiom "Do not strike even with a flower a woman guilty of a hundred crimes" is my rule of conduct.

Balzac.

To be loved as in books is a dream.

Bourget.

The cruellest revenge of a woman is often to remain faithful to a man.

Bossuet.

Women, cats and birds are the creatures that waste most time on their toilets.

Nodier.

Female goodness seldom keeps its ground against laughter, flattery, or fashion.

Johnson.

I received money with her, and for the dowry have sold my authority.

Plautus.

There is no torture that a woman would not suffer to enhance her beauty.

Montaigne.

Most women proceed like the flea, by leaps and jumps.

Balzac.

The most fascinating women are those that can most enrich the every-day moments of existence.

Leigh Hunt.

Learn, above all, how to manage women; their thousand "Ahs" and "Ohs," so thousand fold, can be cured.

Goethe.

All women are fond of minds that inhabit fine bodies, and of souls that have fine eyes.

Joubert.

When women love us, they forgive us everything, even our crimes; when they do not love us, they give us credit for nothing, not even for our virtues.

Balzac.

She who spat in my face while I was, shall come to kiss my feet when I am no more.

Montaigne.

Some women are so just and discerning that they never see an opportunity of being generous.

Anonymous.

I am glad I am not a man, as I should be obliged to marry a woman.

Mme. de Stael.

There would be no such animals as prudes or coquettes in the world were there not such an animal as man.

Addison.

Women have tongues of craft and hearts of guile.

Tasso.

A coquette has no heart; she has only vanity; it is adorers she seeks, not love.

Poincelot.

The reputation of a woman may be compared to a mirror, shining and bright, but liable to be sullied by every breath that comes near it.

Cervantes.

Many men kill themselves for love, but many more women die of it.

———————————

The brain-women never interest us like the heart-women; white roses please less than red.

Holmes.

———————————

A woman is seldom roused to great and courageous exertion, but when something most dear to her is in immediate danger.

Baillie.

———————————

A man can keep another person's secret better than his own; a woman, on the contrary, keeps her secret though she tells all others.

La Bruyère.

———————————

Men speak of what they know; women, of what pleases them.

Rousseau.

———————————

A woman for a general, and the soldiers will be women.

Latin Proverb.

Love is the most terrible, and also the most generous, of the passions; it is the only one which includes in its dreams the happiness of someone else.

Karr.

VIRTUE: a word easy to pronounce, difficult to understand.

Voltaire.

Marriage should combat without respite or mercy that monster that devours everything—habit.

Balzac.

It is easy to find a lover and to retain a friend; what is difficult is to find the friend and retain the lover.

Levis.

It's better to love to-day than to-morrow. A pleasure postponed is a pleasure lost.

Ricard.

Woman conceals only what she does not know.

Proverb.

Love, pleasure, and inconstancy are but the consequences of a desire to know the truth.

Duclos.

A coquette is one that is never to be persuaded out of the passion she has to please, nor out of a good opinion of her own beauty.

Addison.

The vows that woman makes to her fond lover are only fit to be written on air or on the swiftly running stream.

Catullus.

When a *lady* walks the streets, she leaves her virtuous indignation countenance at home.

Holmes.

The humour of affecting a superior carriage generally

115

rises from a false notion of the weakness of the female understanding in general.

Steele.

Woman is mistress of the art of completely embittering the life of the person on whom she depends.

Goethe.

A woman submits to the yoke of opinion, but a man rebels.

De Finod.

The only thing that has been taught successfully to women is to wear becomingly the fig-leaf they received from their first mother.

Diderot.

Woman is like the reed that bends to every breeze, but breaks not in the tempest.

Whately.

Women are happier in the love they inspire than in that

which they feel; men are just the contrary.

De Beauchêne.

To a susceptible youth, like myself, brought up in the country, women are perfect divinities.

Washington Irving.

Women should be careful of their conduct, for appearances sometimes injure them as much as faults.

Girard.

Excess of passion and the force of love, — arguments than which there can be none more powerful to assuage the irritation of a woman's mind.

Titus Livius.

The reason why so few women are touched by friendship is that they find it dull when they have experienced love.

La Rochefoucauld.

Where women are, the better things are implied if not

spoken.

Bronson Alcott.

A woman is a well-served table that one sees with different eyes before and after the meal.

Anonymous.

The materials that go to the making of one woman were set free by the abstraction from inanimate nature of one man's worth of masculine constituents.

Holmes.

Women are wise impromptu, fools on reflection.

Italian Proverb.

To say the truth, I never yet knew a tolerable woman to be fond of her own sex.

Swift.

"I like women," said a clear-headed man of the world, "they are so finished." They finish society, manners, language. Form and ceremony are their realm. They embellish trifles.

Emerson.

———————————

An opinion formed by a woman is inflexible; the fact is not half so stubborn.

Anonymous.

———————————

There is one thing admirable in women; they never reason about their blameworthy actions; even in their dissimulation there is an element of sincerity.

Balzac.

———————————

A mother dreads no memories,—those shadows have all melted away in the dawn of Baby's smiles.

George Eliot.

———————————

Nature has said to woman: Be fair if thou canst, be virtuous if thou wilt; but considerate thou must be.

Beaumarchais.

———————————

A woman either loves or hates; she knows no medium.

Syrus.

The error of certain women is to imagine that, to acquire distinction, they must imitate the manners of men.

De Maistre.

Women's virtue is the music of stringed instruments, which sound best in a room.

Richter.

With women, the desire to bedeck themselves is always the desire to please.

Marmontel.

In life, as in a promenade, woman must lean on a man above her.

Karr.

Kindness in women, not their beauteous looks, shall win my love.

Shakespeare.

The revolution the Boston boys started had to run in mother's milk before it ran in man's blood.

Holmes.

Women swallow at one mouthful the lie that flatters, and drink drop by drop the truth that is bitter.

Diderot.

A shameless woman is the worst of men.

Young.

There has been no church, however superstitious, that has not been adorned by many Christian women devoting their entire lives to assuaging the sufferings of men.

Lecky.

I dare say she's like the rest of the women,—thinks two and two'll come to make five, if she cries and bothers enough about it.

George Eliot.

We need the friendship of a man in great trials, of a woman in the affairs of everyday life.

Thomas.

How can one who hates men love a woman without blushing?

Richter.

Some women need much adorning, as some meat needs much seasoning to incite appetite.

Rochebrune.

'Tis beauty that doth make woman proud;

. . . .

'Tis virtue that doth make them most admired;

. . . .

'Tis government that makes them seem divine.

Shakespeare.

Women like audacity; when one astounds them, he interests them; and when one interests them, he is very sure to please them.

Anonymous.

Women should despise slander, and fear to provoke it.

Mdlle. de Scuderi.

Nature is in earnest when she makes a woman.

Holmes.

However virtuous a woman may be, a compliment on her virtue is what gives her the least pleasure.

Prince de Ligne.

It is not always for virtue's sake that women are virtuous.

La Rochefoucauld.

The society of women is the element of good manners.

Goethe.

Woman is the Sunday of man.

Michelet.

If a woman has any malicious mischief to do, her memory is immortal.

Plautus.

When women have passed thirty, the first thing they forget is their age; when they have attained the age of forty, they have entirely lost the remembrance of it.

De Lenclos.

Even if women were immortal, they could never foresee their last lover.

De Lamennais.

It has been justly observed that heroines are best painted in general terms.

Leigh Hunt.

Love is superior to genius.

De Musset.

Time sooner or later vanquishes love; friendship alone subdues time.

D'Arconville.

A beautiful woman with the qualities of a noble man is the most perfect thing in nature; we find in her all the merits of both sexes.

La Bruyère.

One is alone in a crowd when one suffers, or when one loves.

Rochepedre.

All the passions die with the years; self-love alone never dies.

Voltaire.

A short absence quickens love, a long absence kills it.

Mirabeau.

Marriage often unites for life two people who scarcely know each other.

Balzac.

If a woman refrains from absurd or hateful words and acts, and if she is beautiful, we are straightway convinced that she is a paragon of wisdom and morality.

Tolstoi.

If we men require more perfection from women than

from ourselves, it is doing them honour.

Johnson.

How many women since the days of Echo and Narcissus have pined themselves into air for the love of men who were in love only with themselves.

Anna Jameson.

The castle that parleys and the woman who listens are ready to surrender.

Proverb.

Strange that the Gods should have given an antidote against the venom of savage serpents and none against that of a bad woman.

Euripides.

Women dress less to be clothed than to be adorned. When alone before their mirror they think more of men than of themselves.

Rochebrune.

The woman we love most is often the woman to whom we express it the least.

De Beauchêne.

———————————

Woman's counsel is not worth much, yet he that despises it is no wiser than he should be.

Cervantes.

———————————

Woman is the nervous part of humanity; man the muscular.

Halle.

———————————

O woman, woman! thou art formed to bless the heart of restless man.

Bird.

———————————

Women are often ruined by their sensitiveness and saved by their coquetry.

Mdlle. Azais.

———————————

Women are compounds of plain-sewing and make-believe—daughters of Sham and Hem.

Finesse has been given to woman to compensate the force of man.

De Laclos.

Women are demons who make us enter hell through the gates of paradise.

Anonymous.

It is to teach us early how to think and how to excite our infantile imagination, that prudent nature has given to women so much chit-chat.

La Bruyère.

Oh, woman! woman! thou shouldst have a few sins of thy own to answer for! Thou art the author of such a book of follies in man!

Lytton.

Woman's dignity lies in her being unknown; her glory in the esteem of her husband; and her pleasure in the welfare of her family.

Rousseau.

———————————————

Men *say* of women what pleases them; women *do* with men what pleases them.

Ségur.

———————————————

Woman must not belong to herself; she is bound to alien destinies.

Schiller.

———————————————

Don't trust your horse in the field, nor your wife in your home.

Russian Proverb.

———————————————

Woman has been fed upon flattery until it is not strange she hungers for substantial diet, whose best sauce is understanding and appreciation.

Browne.

———————————————

One thing only I believe in a woman—that she will not come to life again after she is dead.

The life of a woman is a long dissimulation. Candour, beauty, freshness, virginity, modesty,—a woman has each of these but once.

La Bretonne.

Men call physicians only when they suffer; women when they are only afflicted with *ennui*.

Mme. de Genlis.

Men say more evil of a woman than they think; it is the contrary with women toward men.

Dubay.

A woman's rank lies in the fulness of her womanhood; therein alone she is royal.

George Eliot.

The deceit of priests and the cunning of women surpass all else.

Burger.

Nothing is better than a good wife; and nothing is worse than a bad one, who is fond of gadding about.

Hesiod.

Woman often dies for love, as spotless maidens have died to live forever in the pantheon of sentiment.

Browne.

Love, that is but an episode in the life of man, is the entire story of the life of woman.

Mme. de Stael.

Women, priests, and poultry have never enough.

Proverb.

Woman is too soft to hate permanently; even if a hundred men have been a grief to her, she will still love the hundred and first.

Kinkel.

Intellect is to a woman's nature what her skirt is to her dress.

Holmes.

───────────

Without woman man would be rough, rude, solitary, and would ignore all the graces, which are but the smiles of love.

Chateaubriand.

───────────

No woman who is absolutely and entirely good, in the ordinary sense of the word, gets a man's most fervent, passionate love.

Mrs W. K. Clifford.

───────────

It is a misfortune for a woman never to be loved, but it is a humiliation to be loved no more.

Montesquieu.

───────────

Woman is the salvation or the destruction of the family.

Amiel.

───────────

An old coquette has all the defects of a young one, and

none of her charms.

———————————

Women, like the plants in the woods, derive their softness and tenderness from the shade.

Landor.

———————————

One should choose a wife with the ears rather than with the eyes.

Proverb.

———————————

From many a woman's fortune this truth is clear as day; that falsely smiling pleasure with pain requites us ever.

Nibelungenlied.

———————————

Half the sorrows of women would be averted if they could repress the speech they know to be useless,—nay, the speech they have resolved not to utter.

George Eliot.

———————————

Men know that women are an over-match for them,

and therefore choose the weakest and most ignorant.

Johnson.

Woman's sensibility lights up, and quivers and falls, like the flame of a coal fire.

Mitchell.

The weakness of women gives to some men a victory that their merit would never gain.

Anonymous.

Women like brave men exceedingly, but audacious men still more.

Le Mesle.

The mistake of many women is to return sentiment for gallantry.

Jouy.

Women can rarely be deceived, for they are accustomed to deceive.

Aristophanes.

There are no pleasures where women are not.

Marie De Romieu.

Women's tender hearts are much more susceptible of good impressions than the minds of the other sex.

Steele.

Coquettes are like hunters who are fond of hunting, but do not eat the game.

Anonymous.

Marriage with a good woman is a harbour in the tempest; but with a bad woman, it proves a tempest in the harbour.

Petit-Senn.

A man without religion is to be pitied, but a godless woman is a horror above all things.

Elizabeth Evans.

Cruelly tempted, perplexed and bewildered, when passion is stronger than reason, women do not think of consequences, but go blindfolded, headlong to their ruin.

Amelia E. Barr.

———————

Vanity acts like a woman,—they both think they lose something when love or praise is accorded to another.

Anonymous.

———————

One woman reads another's character without the tedious trouble of deciphering.

Ben Jonson.

———————

Women are much more like each other than men; they have, in truth, but two passions,—vanity and love.

Chesterfield.

———————

A jest that makes a virtuous woman only smile, often frightens away a prude.

De Latena.

———————

If the loving closed heart of a good woman were to open before a man, how much controlled tenderness, how many veiled sacrifices and dumb virtues would he see!

Richter.

There are twenty-four hours in a day, and not a moment in the twenty-four in which a woman may not change her mind.

De Finod.

Most women are better out of their houses than in them.

Tacitus.

How many women are born too finely organised in sense and soul for the highway; they must walk with feet unshod!

Holmes.

Women are rakes by nature and prudes by necessity.

La Rochefoucauld.

What means did the devil find out, or what instrument did his own subtlety present him, as fittest and aptest to work his mischief by? Even the unquiet vanity of the woman.

Sir Walter Raleigh.

An obscure mist of sighs exhales out of the solitude of women in the nineteenth century.

Alger.

If a woman's young and pretty, I think you can see her good looks all the better for her being plainly dressed.

George Eliot.

A man is in general better pleased when he has a good dinner than when his wife talks Greek.

Johnson.

A young girl betrays, in a moment, that her eyes have been feeding on the face where you find them fixed.

Holmes.

Life is not long enough for a coquette to play all her tricks in.

Addison.

━━━━━━━━━━━

The woman who loves us is only a woman, but the woman we love is a celestial being, whose defects disappear under the prism through which we see her.

Girardin.

━━━━━━━━━━━

Woman's love, like lichens on a rock, will still grow where even charity can find no soil to nurture itself.

Bovée.

━━━━━━━━━━━

If a fox is cunning, a woman in love is still more so.

Proverb.

━━━━━━━━━━━

There are few husbands whom the wife cannot win in the long run by patience and love.

Marguerite de Valois.

━━━━━━━━━━━

A woman indeed ventures most, for she hath no sanctuary to retire to from an evil husband.

Jeremy Taylor.

———————

Better to have never loved, than to have loved unhappily, or to have *half* loved.

Louise Colet.

———————

Love makes time pass, and time makes love pass.

Proverb.

———————

Love is the passion of great souls; it makes them merit glory, when it does not turn their heads.

De Pompadour.

———————

Nothing is so embarrassing as the first *tête-à-tête,* when there is everything to say, unless it be the last, when everything has been said.

Roqueplan.

———————

All joys do not cause laughter; great pleasures are serious; pleasures of love do not make us laugh.

Voltaire.

The beautiful is always severe.

Ségur.

Love! Love! Eternal enigma! Will not the Sphinx that guards thee find an Ædipus to explain thee?

Pyat.

Friendship between two women is always a plot against each other.

Karr.

Divert your mistress rather than sigh for her.

Steele.

The ever-womanly draws us above.

Goethe.

I love men, not because they are men, but because they are not women.

Queen Christina.

Flow, wine! smile, women! and the universe is consoled.

Beranger.

Discretion is more necessary to women than eloquence, because they have less trouble to speak well than to speak little.

Du Bose.

There is no gown or garment that worse becomes a woman than when she will be wise.

Luther.

Women live only in the emotion that love gives.

Houssaye.

On great occasions it is almost always women who have given the strongest proofs of virtue and devotion.

Montholon.

God bless all good women! To their soft hands and

pitying hearts we must all come at last.

Holmes.

Neither education nor reason gives women much security against the influence of example.

Johnson.

The hell for women who are only handsome is old age.

Saint-Evremond.

Men are women's playthings, women are the devil's.

Victor Hugo.

A woman, if she is bent on ill, never goes begging to the gardener for material; she has a garden at home.

Plautus.

The woman in us still prosecutes a deceit like that begun in the garden; and our understandings are wedded to an Eve as fatal as the mother of their miseries.

Glanvill.

Among all animals, from man to the dog, the heart of a mother is always a sublime thing.

Dumas.

There are no ugly women; there are only women who do not know how to look pretty.

Berryer.

It is not for good women that men have fought battles, given their lives, and staked their souls.

Mrs W. K. Clifford.

Women's sympathies give a tone, like the harp of Æolus, to the slightest breath.

Mitchell.

A coquette is a woman who places her honour in a lottery; ninety-nine chances to one that she will lose it.

Anonymous.

145

The honour of woman is badly guarded when it is guarded by keys and spies. No woman is honest who does not wish to be.

Dupuy.

The man that lays his hand upon a woman, save in the way of kindness, is a wretch whom 'twere gross flattery to name a coward.

Tobin.

Beauty deceives women in making them establish on an ephemeral power the pretensions of a whole life.

De Bigincourt.

I do not know that she was virtuous; but she was ugly, and with a woman that is half the battle.

Heine.

Love works miracles every day; such as weakening the strong and strengthening the weak; making fools of the wise, and wise men of fools; favouring the passions, destroying reason, and, in a word, turning everything topsy-turvy.

Marguerite de Valois.

In love, as in everything else, experience is a physician who never comes until after the disorder is cured.

De la Tour.

Those who always speak well of women do not know them enough; those who always speak ill of them do not know them at all.

Pigault-Lebrun.

Were we perfectly acquainted with our idol, we should never passionately desire it.

La Rochefoucauld.

Love is like the moon; when it does not increase, it decreases.

Ségur.

As soon as women are ours, we are no longer theirs.

Montaigne.

A woman laughs when she can, and weeps when she will.

Proverb.

Woman may complain to God, as subjects do of tyrant princes; but otherwise she hath no appeal in the causes of unkindness.

Jeremy Taylor.

A bachelor seeks a wife to avoid solitude; a married man seeks society to avoid a *tête-à-tête*.

Varennes.

Silence and blushing are the eloquence of women.

Chinese Proverb.

A woman who has not seen her lover for the whole day considers that day lost for her; the tenderest of men consider it only lost for love.

Madame de Salm.

A woman that is ill-treated has no refuge in her griefs

but in silence and secrecy.

Steele.

There are only two good women in the world; one of them is dead, and the other is not to be found.

German Proverb.

The most beautiful object in the world, it will be allowed, is a beautiful woman.

Macaulay.

No woman can be handsome by the force of features alone, any more than she can be witty only by the help of speech.

Hughes.

Every pretty girl one sees is a reminiscence of the Garden of Eden.

Sheldon.

The Marys who bring ointment for our feet get but little thanks.

Thackeray.

———————

We censure the inconstancy of women when we are the victims; we find it charming when we are the objects.

Desnoyers.

———————

The purer the golden vessel the more readily is it bent; the higher worth of women is sooner lost than that of men.

Richter.

———————

Nature has given beauty to women which can resist shields and spears. She who is beautiful is stronger than iron and flame.

Anacreon.

———————

The heart of true womanhood knows where its own sphere is, and never seeks to stray beyond it.

Hawthorne.

———————

Millions of people, generations of slaves, perish in this penal servitude of the factories merely in order to satisfy the whim of woman.

Tolstoi.

A woman of sense ought to be above flattering any man.

Holmes.

The reason why so few marriages are happy is because young ladies spend their time making nets, not cages.

Anonymous.

Woman knows that the better she obeys the surer she is to rule.

Michelet.

I have found that there is an intimate connection between the character of women and the fancy that makes them choose such and such material.

Prosper Merimée.

Woman is the most perfect when the most womanly.

Gladstone.

Woman is at once apple and serpent.

Heine.

One must have loved a woman of genius in order to comprehend what happiness there is in loving a fool.

Talleyrand.

The most reasonable women have hours wherein to be unreasonable.

Cherbuliez.

The love of a bad woman kills others; the love of a good and noble woman kills herself.

George Sand.

Woman is born for love, and it is impossible to turn her from seeking it.

Ossoli.

Man sometimes asks of a book the truth; a woman

always her illusions.

Goncourt.

Societies commence with polygamy and finish with polyandry.

Goncourt.

In a truly loving heart either jealousy kills love or love kills jealousy.

Bourget.

It is not the treachery of women, but our own, which makes us beware of them.

Bourget.

The world either breaks or hardens the heart.

Chamfort.

A mother's tenderness and caresses are the milk of the heart.

De Guerin.

Great vices, and great virtues, are exceptions in mankind.

Napoleon I.

Most women caress sin before embracing penitence.

Durois-Fontanelle.

When Eve ate the apple she knew she was naked. I have often thought, as I looked at her dancing daughters, that another bite would be of service to them.

Sheldon.

Woman is a creature between man and the angels.

Balzac.

Education raises many poor women to a stage of refinement that makes them suitable companions for men of a higher rank, and not suitable for those of their own.

Lecky.

Elegance of appearance, ornaments, and dress, these are women's badges of distinction; in these they delight and glory.

Titus Livius.

Men who paint sylphs, fall in love with some *bonne et brave femme*, heavy-heeled and freckled.

George Eliot.

Woman—the gods be thanked!—is not even collaterally related to that sentimental abstraction called an angel.

Browne.

There will always remain something to be said of woman, as long as there is one on the earth.

Boufflers.

There are no oaths that make so many perjurers as the vows of love.

Rochebrune.

The heart makes of woman a sublime being, the senses

in their brutality make of her a true being.

Bourget.

It is neither honour nor love which makes a betrayed man think of killing a woman. Murder comes of the senses.

Bourget.

Love is a religion and its cult must cost more than that of all the other religions.

Bourget.

Of an ancient love one may make everything, even a new love—everything, except friendship.

Bourget.

One blushes oftener from the wounds of self-love than from modesty.

Guibert.

When the intoxication of love has passed, we laugh at the perfections it had discovered.

De Lenclos.

———————

The passions are the orators of great assemblies.

Rivarol.

———————

Every one speaks well of his heart, but no one dares to speak well of his mind.

La Rochefoucauld.

———————

There are people who are *almost* in love, *almost* famous, and *almost* happy.

De Krudener.

———————

Women are an aristocracy.

Michelet.

———————

Women are too imaginative and sensitive to have much logic.

Mme. du Deffand.

———————

The man who lives in indifference is one who has never seen the woman he could love.

La Bruyère.

———————————

I wish Adam had died with all his ribs in his body.

Boucicault.

———————————

One mother is more venerable than a thousand fathers.

Laws of Manu.

———————————

Tell a woman that she is beautiful, and the devil will repeat it to her ten times.

Italian Proverb.

———————————

A woman is most merciless when shame goads on her hate.

Juvenal.

———————————

God made her small in order to do a more choice bit of workmanship.

De Musset.

The venom of the female viper is more poisonous than that of the male viper.

Butler.

Friendships of women are cushions wherein they stick their pins.

Anonymous.

Women rouge that they may not blush.

Italian Proverb.

A woman in love is a very poor judge of character.

Holland.

There was never yet fair woman but she made mouths in a glass.

Shakespeare.

A woman's whole life is the history of the affections. The heart is her world; it is there her ambition strives for empire.

Washington Irving.

———————————————

Women never lie more astutely than when they tell the truth to those who do not believe them.

Anonymous.

———————————————

A woman's friendship borders more closely on love than man's.

Coleridge.

———————————————

Women never weep more bitterly than when they weep with spite.

Ricard.

———————————————

To love her is a liberal education.

Congreve.

———————————————

It is to woman that the heart appeals when it needs consolation.

Demoustier.

Irregular vivacity of temper leads astray the hearts of ordinary women in the choice of their lovers and the treatment of their husbands.

Addison.

A woman without beauty knows but half of life.

Mme. de Montaran.

The only confidence that one can repose in the most discreet woman is the confidence of her beauty.

Le Mesle.

A knot of ladies got together by themselves is a very school of impertinence and detraction, and it is well if those be the worst.

Swift.

Never say man, but men; nor women, but woman; for the world has thousands of men and only one woman.

Weiss.

But one thing on earth is better than the wife—that is
the mother.

Schefer.

A virtuous woman has in the heart a fibre less or a fibre
more than other women; she is stupid or sublime.

Balzac.

In every loving woman there is a priestess of the past.

Amiel.

All women are good—good for nothing, or good for
something.

Cervantes.

Women are a new race, re-created since the world
received Christianity.

Henry Ward Beecher.

Beauty, in a modest woman, is like fire or a sharp sword
at a distance: neither doth the one burn nor the other
wound those that come not too near them.

Cervantes.

What woman desires is written in heaven.

La Chaussée.

Woman is the highest, holiest, most precious gift to man. Her mission and throne is the family.

Todd.

Of all heavy bodies, the heaviest is the woman we have ceased to love.

Lemontey.

If a wife can induce herself to submit patiently to her husband's mode of life, she will have no difficulty to manage him.

Aristotle.

Men would be saints if they loved God as they love women.

St Thomas.

Than woman there is no fouler and viler fiend when her mind is bent on ill.

Homer.

A woman forgives everything but the fact that you do not covet her.

De Musset.

The desire to please is born in women before the desire to love.

De Lenclos.

Of all things that man possesses, women alone take pleasure in being possessed.

Malherbe.

Women and young men are apt to tell what secrets they know from the vanity of having been trusted.

Chesterfield.

164

Women are like pictures; of no value in the hands of a fool, till he hears men of sense bid high for the purchase.

Farquhar.

The best woman is the one least talked about.

Schiller.

In this advanced century a girl of sixteen knows as much as her mother, and enjoys her knowledge much more.

Anonymous.

In love, a woman is like a lyre that surrenders its secrets only to the hand that knows how to touch its strings.

Balzac.

Men say knowledge is power; women think dress is power.

Sheldon.

She is the most virtuous woman whom Nature has

made the most voluptuous, and reason the coldest.

La Beaumelle.

―――――――

For one woman who affronts her kind by wicked passions or remorseless hate, a thousand make amends in age and youth.

Mackay.

―――――――

It is often woman who inspires us with the great things that she will prevent us from accomplishing.

Dumas.

―――――――

A man who is known to have broken many hearts is naturally invested with a tantalising charm to women who have yet hearts to be broken.

Boyesen.

―――――――

Between a woman's "yes" and "no" I would not venture to stick a pin.

Cervantes.

―――――――

A woman's love is often a misfortune; her friendship is

always a boon.

Mézières.

A woman's head is always influenced by her heart, but a man's heart is always influenced by his head.

Blessington.

Women love always; when earth slips away from them they take refuge in heaven.

Anonymous.

The finger of the first woman loved is like that of God: the imprint of it is eternal.

Anonymous.

Most women prefer that we should talk ill of their virtue rather than of their wit or of their beauty.

Fontenelle.

In buying horses and in taking a wife, shut your eyes tight and commend yourself to God.

Tuscan Proverb.

All women desire to be esteemed; they care much less about being respected.

Dumas.

Women are women but to become mothers: they go to duty through pleasure.

Joubert.

Coquetry is a net laid by the vanity of women to ensnare that of man.

Bruin.

To a woman of delicate feeling, the most persuasive declaration of love is the embarrassment of an intellectual man.

De Latena.

A coquette is to a man what a toy is to a child; as long as it pleases him he keeps it.

Anonymous.

When a woman once begins to be ashamed of what she ought not to be ashamed of, she will not be ashamed of what she ought.

Titus Livius.

———————————

Friend, beware of fair maidens! When their tenderness begins, our servitude is near.

Victor Hugo.

———————————

That perfect disinterestedness and self-devotion of which man seems incapable, but which is sometimes found in women.

Macaulay.

———————————

A pretty woman's worth some pains to see.

Browning.

———————————

If you wish a coquette to regard you, cease to regard her.

Anonymous.

———————————

Women of forty always fancy they have found the

Fountain of Youth, and that they remain young in the midst of the ruins of their day.

Houssaye.

───────────────

The perfect loveliness of a woman's countenance can only consist in that majestic peace which is founded in the memory of happy and useful years, full of sweet records.

Ruskin.

───────────────

Trust your dog to the end; a woman—till the first opportunity.

Proverb.

───────────────

In mythology no god falls in love with Minerva. A mannish woman only attracts a feminine man.

Sheldon.

───────────────

Women have the same desires as men, but do not have the same right to express them.

Rousseau.

───────────────

Youth feeds on its own flowery pastures; in pleasures it builds up a life that knows no trouble till the name of virgin is lost in that of wife.

Sophocles.

———————————

The world is so unjust that a female heart which has once been touched is thought for ever blemished.

Steele.

———————————

Nature and custom would, no doubt, agree in conceding to all males the right of at least two distinct looks at every comely female countenance.

Holmes.

———————————

We love handsome women from inclination, homely women from interest, and virtuous women from reason.

Houssaye.

———————————

There is something still more to be studied than a Jesuit, and that is a Jesuitess.

Eugene Sue.

———————————

Uneducated men may escape intellectual degradation;
uneducated women cannot.

Sydney Smith.

A woman and her servant, acting in accord, would
outwit a dozen devils.

Proverb.

Cast in so slight and exquisite a mould, so mild and
gentle, so pure and beautiful, that earth seemed not her
element, nor its rough creatures her fit companions.

Dickens.

The wife is a constellation of virtues; she's the moon,
and thou art the man in the moon.

Congreve.

Scylla must have broken off many excellent matches in
her time, if she insisted upon all that loved her loving
her dogs also.

Lamb.

A light wife doth make a heavy husband.

Shakespeare.

Trust a poor woman to dress her children in finery.

Mitchell.

A woman is turned into a love-magnet by a tingling current of life running around her.

Holmes.

Women and maidens must be praised, whether truly or falsely.

German Proverb.

The supreme beauty of Greek art is rather male than female.

Winckelmann.

The man is the head of the woman, but she rules him by her temper.

Russian Proverb.

Women are in general more addicted to the petty forms of vanity, jealousy, spitefulness, and ambition, and they are also inferior to men in active courage.

Lecky.

Certain importunities always please women, even when the importuner does not please.

Anonymous.

It is difficult for a woman ever to try to be anything good when she is not believed in,—when it is always supposed that she must be contemptible.

George Eliot.

Woman's beauty, the forest's echo, and rainbows soon pass away.

German Proverb.

The starry crown of woman is in the power of her affection and sentiment and the infinite enlargements to which they lead.

Emerson.

However much woman may need deliverance from some outward trials and disabilities, her grand want is a freer, deeper, richer, holier inward life.

Alger.

He that hath a fair wife never wants trouble.

Proverb.

The man who awakes the wondering, trembling passion of a young girl always thinks her affectionate.

George Eliot.

A woman, unlike Narcissus, seeks not her own image and a second I; she much prefers a not I.

Richter.

Woman is seldom merciful to the man who is timid.

Lytton.

A wife! A mother! Two magical words, comprising the

sweetest source of man's felicity. Theirs is the reign of beauty, of love, of reason, — always a reign.

Aimi Martin.

———————————

Woman is the dwelling-place of religion, and communicates it to the young.

Channing.

———————————

The first and chief thing that should be looked for in a woman is fear.

Tolstoi.

———————————

A woman fascinates a man quite as often by what she overlooks as by what she sees.

Holmes.

———————————

Women have no fear of marriage, because they are so occupied in imagining the happiness it may bring them that they never think of the possible misery it includes.

Anonymous.

———————————

Devotion is the last love of women.

Saint-Evremond.

A woman with whom one discusses love is always in expectation of something.

Poincelot.

The beauty of some women has days and seasons, and depends upon accidents which diminish or increase it.

Cervantes.

We meet in society many attractive women whom we would fear to make our wives.

D'Harleville.

The woman who plays with the love of a loyal man is a curse; she may close his heart for ever against all confidence in her sex.

Anonymous.

It is the male that gives charm to womankind, that produces an air in their faces, a grace in their motions, a softness in their voices, and a delicacy in their complexions.

Addison.

In life, woman must wait until she is asked to love, as in a salon she waits for an invitation to dance.

Karr.

A sharp eye can almost always see the train leading from a young girl's eye or lip to the "I love you" in her heart.

Holmes.

Women, wind, and fortune soon change.

Spanish Proverb.

A woman without a laugh in her ... is the greatest bore in nature.

Thackeray.

To women, mildness is the best means to be right.

Mme. de Fontaines.

Women bestow on friendship only what they borrow from love.

Chamfort.

The best shelter for a girl is her mother's wing.

Anonymous.

Whoever, allured by riches or high rank, marries a vicious woman is a fool.

Euripides.

For a woman to be at once a coquette and a bigot is more than the meekest of husbands can bear.

La Bruyère.

A wretched woman is more unfortunate than a wretched man.

Victor Hugo.

A good woman is a hidden treasure; who discovers her will do well not to boast about it.

La Rochefoucauld.

Women are twice as religious as men; all the world knows that.

Holmes.

The most dreadful thing against women is the character of the men who praise them.

Anonymous.

—————————————

A woman is naturally as much more capricious than a man as she is more susceptible. A slighter shock suffices to jostle her delicate emotions out of delight into disgust.

Alger.

—————————————

Love thy wife as thy soul; shake her as a plum-tree.

Russian Proverb.

—————————————

Love is of all the passions the strongest, for it attacks simultaneously the head, the heart, and the senses.

Voltaire.

—————————————

Time is the sovereign physician of all passions.

Montaigne.

—————————————

Obstacles usually stimulate passion, but sometimes they kill it.

Sand.

Folly was condemned to serve as a guide to Love whom she had blinded.

La Fontaine.

The future of society is in the hands of the mothers. If the world was lost through woman, she alone can save it.

De Beaufort.

The breaking of a heart leaves no traces.

Sand.

From the moment it is touched, the heart cannot dry up.

Bourdaloue.

'Tis the greatest misfortune in nature for a woman to want a confidant.

Farquhar.

How many women would laugh at the funerals of their husbands if it were not the custom to weep.

Anonymous.

Venus with ease engenders wiles in knowing dames; but a woman of simple capacity, by reason of her small understanding, is removed from folly.

Euripides.

Modesty in women has great advantages; it enhances beauty, and serves as a veil to uncomeliness.

Fontenelle.

Of all wild beasts, on earth or in the sea, the greatest is a woman.

Anonymous.

One must tell women only what one wants to be known.

Beaumarchais.

Speak to women in a style and manner proper to approach them, they never fail to improve by your counsels.

Steele.

A woman without religion is even worse, a flame without heat, a rainbow without colour, a flower without perfume.

Mitchell.

A woman once fallen will shrink from no impropriety.

Tacitus.

I don't want a woman to weigh me in a balance; there are men enough for that sort of work.

Holmes.

Women soften our character, and yet make us heroic. The same traits of character produce these different effects.

Channing.

Women, like empresses, condemn to imprisonment and hard labour nine-tenths of mankind.

Tolstoi.

━━━━━━━━━━━━━━

There is one dangerous science for women, one which let them indeed beware how they profanely touch; that of theology.

Ruskin.

━━━━━━━━━━━━━━

A woman's fame is the tomb of her happiness.

Proverb.

━━━━━━━━━━━━━━

There will be so many more women in heaven than men that any marriage, except of the Mormon kind, would be impossible.

Sheldon.

━━━━━━━━━━━━━━

COQUETTE—a female general who builds her fame on her advances.

Field.

━━━━━━━━━━━━━━

When, like spoiled children, women cry for the moon, it

185

is because they have heard that the moon contains a man.

Browne.

Women famed for their valour, their skill in politics, or their learning, leave the duties of their own sex in order to invade the privileges of ours.

Goldsmith.

Woman is fine for her own satisfaction alone; man only knows man's insensibility to a new gown.

Jane Austen.

Women in this degenerate age are rare, to whom aught else but sordid gain is dear.

Ariosto.

Woman, divorced from home, wanders unfriended like a waif upon the waves.

Goethe.

Women are right to crave beauty at any price, since

beauty is the only merit that men do not contest with them.

Dupuy.

––––––––––––––––––

Your true flirt plays with sparkles; her heart, much as there is of it, spends itself in sparkles; she measures it to sparkle, and habit grows into nature.

Mitchell.

––––––––––––––––––

The prejudices of men emanate from the mind, and may be overcome; the prejudices of women emanate from the heart, and are impregnable.

Boyer d'Argens.

––––––––––––––––––

Women are the poetry of the world in the same sense as the stars are the poetry of heaven.

Hargrave.

––––––––––––––––––

The pleasure of talking is the inextinguishable passion of women, coeval with the act of breathing.

Lesage.

––––––––––––––––––

Women of the world never use harsh expressions when condemning their rivals.

Anonymous.

Women are, for the most part, good or bad, as they fall amongst those who practise virtue or vice.

Johnson.

Women exceed the generality of men in love.

La Bruyère.

Women commend a modest man, and like him not.

Proverb.

A delicate woman is the best instrument; she has such a magnificent compass of sensibilities.

Holmes.

To say "Everyone is talking about him" is a eulogy; but to say "Everyone is talking about her" is an elegy.

Anonymous.

Curiosity is one of the forms of feminine bravery.

Victor Hugo.

Confound the make-believe women we have turned loose in our streets.

Holmes.

It is easier to take care of a peck of fleas than of one woman.

Proverb.

Women are like thermometers, which, on a sudden application of heat, sink at first a few degrees, as preliminary to rising a good many.

Richter.

Until we know woman, we know not *strength of love.* In this we have, perhaps, the best emblem of omnipotence as well as divine goodness.

Channing.

A coquette sparkles, but it is more the sparkle of a harmless and pretty vanity than of calculation.

Mitchell.

Her step is music, and her voice is song.

Bailey.

Man carves his destiny; woman is helped to hers.

Julia Ward Howe.

If the women did not make idols of us, and if they saw us as we see each other, would life be bearable or could society go on?

Thackeray.

Women are apt to love the men who they think have the largest capacity of loving.

Holmes.

There are few women whose charms survive their beauty.

La Rochefoucauld.

A woman despises a man for loving her unless she happens to return his love.

Elizabeth Stoddard.

Beauty is the first gift Nature gives to woman, and the first she takes from her.

De Méré.

Women must have their wills while they live, because they make none when they die.

Proverb.

Women never truly command till they have given their promise to obey; and they are never in more danger of being made slaves than when the men are at their feet.

Farquhar.

A woman who is guided by the head, and not by the heart, is a social pestilence.

Balzac.

An asp would render its sting more venomous by dipping it into the heart of a coquette.

Poincelot.

Voluptuaries know what they talk about when they profess not to care for sense in woman.

Leigh Hunt.

A woman who has surrendered her lips has surrendered everything.

Viaud.

A woman repents sincerely of her fault only after being weaned from her infatuation for the one who induced her to commit it.

De Latena.

Let the great soul incarnated in some woman's form, poor and sad and single, in some Dolly or Joan, go out to service.

Emerson.

Woman, naturally enthusiastic of the good and beautiful, sanctifies all that she surrounds with her affection.

Mercier.

Woman have more understanding than we have, and women of spirit are not to be won by mourners.

Steele.

Marry a virgin, that thou mayst teach her discreet manners.

Hesiod.

Pretty women gaze at a beauty with envy, homely women with spite, old men with regret, young men with transport.

D'Argens.

Hell is paved with women's tongues.

Abbé Guyon.

A woman is more influenced by what she divines than

by what she is told.

De Lenclos.

We never fall in love with a woman, in distinction from women, until we can get an image of her through a pinhole.

Holmes.

However talkative a woman may be, love teaches her silence.

Rochebrune.

There is something so gross in the carriage of some wives that they lose their husbands' hearts.

Budgell.

Men declare their love before they feel it; women confess theirs only after they have proved it.

De Latena.

In love it is only the commencement that charms. I am not surprised that one finds pleasure in frequently recommencing.

Prince de Ligne.

The heart of a loving woman is a golden sanctuary, where often there reigns an idol of clay.

Limayrae.

Women call repentance the sweet remembrance of their faults and the bitter regret of their inability to recommence them.

Beaumanoir.

Virtue, with some women, is but the precaution of locking doors.

Lemontey.

She had married her husband for his wit, and was willing to do the next best thing for any man who was wittier.

Francis Prevost.

Women are often ruined by their sensitiveness and

saved by their coquetry.

Mdlle. Azaïs.

In love only the awkward are punished—like the Spartan thieves.

Anonymous.

The action of woman on our destiny is unceasing.

Lord Beaconsfield.

The weaknesses of women have been given them by nature to exercise the virtues of men.

Mme. Necker.

The most chaste woman may be the most voluptuous, if she loves.

Mirabeau.

Love renders chaste the most voluptuous pleasures.

Virey.

Manners, morals, customs change: the passions are always the same.

Mme. de Flahaut.

Discretion is more necessary to women than eloquence.

Du Bosc.

Marriage is a lottery in which men stake their liberty, and women their happiness.

Mme. de Rieux.

Orpheus went to Hell to find his wife: how many widowers would not even go to Heaven to find theirs?

Petit-Senn.

When a lover gives, he demands—and much more than he has given.

Parny.

A reputation for success has as much influence with women as a reputation for wealth has with men.

Lord Beaconsfield.

Women give themselves to God when the Devil wants nothing more to do with them.

Sophie Arnould.

The beauty of a young girl should speak to the imagination, and not to the senses.

Karr.

Prudery is the hypocrisy of modesty.

Massias.

Women distrust men too much in general, and not enough in particular.

Commerson.

There is a magic in Duty which sustains judges, inflames warriors and cools the married.

Dupuy.

There are beautiful flowers that are scentless, and

beautiful women that are unlovable.

Hovellé.

Love is a beggar who still begs when one has given him everything.

Rochepedre.

The quarrels of lovers are like summer showers that leave the country more verdant and beautiful.

Mme. Necker.

The desire to please is born in woman before the desire to love.

De Lenclos.

A prude ought to be condemned to meet only indiscreet lovers.

Raisson.

Science seldom renders men amiable; women never.

Beauchêne.

Women are in the moral world what flowers are in the physical.

Maréchal.

Who loves not women, wine and song, remains a fool his whole life long.

Martin Luther.

Virtue and Love are two ogres: one must eat the other.

D'Houdetot.

Love never dies of starvation, but often of indigestion.

De Lenclos.

Women swallow at one mouthful the lie that flatters, and drink drop by drop a truth that is bitter.

Diderot.

A woman with whom one discusses love is always in expectation of something.

Poincelot.

The society of women endangers men's morals and refines their manners.

Montesquieu.

Love pleases more than marriage, for the reason that romance is more interesting than history.

Chamfort.

Fortune hath somewhat of the nature of a woman, who, if she be too closely wooed, is commonly the further off.

Charles V.

Great pleasures are serious: pleasures of love do not make us laugh.

Voltaire.

One is always a woman's first lover.

De Laclos.

Even if women were immortal, they could never foresee their last lover.

Lammenais.

Devotion is the last love of women.

St Evremond.

Love, that sometimes corrupts pure bodies, often purifies corrupt hearts.

Laténa.

Coquetry is a continual lie, which renders a woman more contemptible and more dangerous than a courtesan who never lies.

De Varennes.

Marriage is often but ennui for two.

Commerson.

Love that seldom gives us happiness, at least makes us

dream of it.

Sénancourt.

Woman is the most precious jewel taken from Nature's casket for the ornamentation and happiness of man.

Guyard.

Marriage is a feast where the grace is sometimes better than the dinner.

Lacon.

Love is like medical science—the art of assisting Nature.

Lallemand.

To continue love in marriage is a science.

Mme. Reyband.

The mistake of many women is to return sentiment for gallantry.

Jouy.

It is not love that ruins us; it is the way we make it.

Bussy-Rabutin.

———————————

Marriage in our days?—I would almost say that it is a rape by contract.

Michelet.

———————————

A coquette often loses her reputation while she possesses her virtue.

Spectator.

———————————

A lover is a man who endeavours to be more amiable than it is possible for him to be: this is the reason why almost all lovers are ridiculous.

Chamfort.

———————————

Those who always speak well of women do not know them enough; those who always speak ill of them do not know them at all.

Pigault-Lebrun.

———————————

Possession is the touchstone of love.

Beauty is the first gift Nature gives to woman, and the first she takes from her.

Méré.

It is a terrible thing to be obliged to love by contract.

Bussy-Rabutin.

Our strong passions break into a thousand purposes; women have one.

Lord Beaconsfield.

Women alone can organise a drawing-room: man succeeds sometimes in a library.

Lord Beaconsfield.

Male firmness is very often obstinacy. Women have always something better, worth all qualities. They have tact.

Lord Beaconsfield.

The woman who is talked about is generally virtuous, and she is only abused because she devotes to *one* the charms which all wish to enjoy.

Lord Beaconsfield.

There is no mortification, however keen, no misery, however desperate, which the spirit of woman cannot in some degree lighten or alleviate.

Lord Beaconsfield.

The affections are the children of ignorance; when the horizon of our experience expands, and models multiply, love and admiration imperceptibly vanish.

Lord Beaconsfield.

Where there are crowned heads there are always some charming women.

Lord Beaconsfield.

There is nothing a man of good sense dreads in a wife so much as her having more sense than himself.

Fielding.

It is only a woman that can make a man become the parody of himself.

French Proverb.

There will always remain something to be said of woman, as long as there is one on the earth.

Boufflers.

The End